TAILS

A BOOK OF IDENTIFYING ANIMAL TAILS

BY BARBARA AND TAYLOR PAPA

LCCN: 2025911882
ISBN Hardcover: 978-1-968404-06-2

A

I swim in fresh water
and I like to lay in the sun

I can run very fast when
I swing my tail back
and forth

My snout is round in shape
and I have very sharp teeth

What Animal
Am I?

ALLIGATOR

B

I can live in the water or
on land

I have a flat tail that helps
me build dams to collect
water, and for protection

I eat soft leaves, twigs and
bark from trees. I also love
soft shrubs and apples

What Animal
Am I?

BEAVER

C

I like to catch mice

I like to chase birds

I say MEOW

What Animal
Am I?

CAT

D

I like to chase balls

I like to chew on bones

I say Woof & Bark

What Animal
Am I?

DOG

E

I like to eat peanuts

I have a long trunk

I love to sit in the water
And mud to cool off

What Animal
Am I?

ELEPHANT

F

I am pink in color
And have long legs

I like to live in Florida

I like to eat shrimp
and insects with my
curved Bill

What Animal
am I?

FLAMINGO

G

I am the tallest animal
in the world

I love to eat leaves off
the trees

I have a spotted body with
a very long neck and legs

What Animal
Am I?

GIRAFFE

H

I am very big with short
legs, a tail and a BIG
mouth

I love sitting in the water

I eat plants and other
Vegetation in the water

What Animal
am I?

HIPPOPOTAMUS

I

I live in warm climates

I can change color to
blend in with my
surroundings

I can grow up to 6 feet,
have a long tail and toes

What Animal
Am I?

IGUANA

J

I am the largest cat in
The Americas

I can be yellow or orange
with black spots

I like to eat meat

What Animal
am I?

JAGUAR

K

I live mostly in Australia

I can hop very high
and far

I carry my babies in my
front pouch

What Animal
am I?

KANGAROO

L

I am called King of the
Jungle

I have a big furry mane
around my face

I can weigh up to 500
pounds

What Animal
Am I?

LION

M

I am tall and skinny
with large eyes and
a pointed snout

I live in burrowed holes
and come from Africa

I love to eat beetles

What Animal
Am I?

MEERKAT

N

I am similar to a
salamander

I am called an Eft as
a youngster, when I
can only live on land

When I become an adult,
I spend most of my time
in the water

What Animal
Am I?

NEWT

O

I a very tall bird with a
long neck and big beak

I have long fluffy feathers

I can run faster than
a man

What Animal
am I?

OSTRICH

P

I have long sharp
needles on my body
called Quills

I use my Quills to
defend myself

I am a very good
swimmer and like
to climb trees

What Animal
am I?

PORCUPINE

Q

I am a small little fat
bird with a plume on
on my head

I lay a lot of eggs at
one time

I like to live mostly in
California and Arizona

What Animal
Am I?

QUAIL

R

I am in the rodent
family

I love going through
trash cans for food

I have large eyes and
big ears

What Animal
am I?

RAT

S

I can be short or long
and many colors

I love slithering through
grass, bushes and rocks

One type of me even has
a rattle on its head

What Animal
am I?

SNAKE

T

I am very large with
black and orange stripes

I am in the cat family

I can roar and climb
trees to sleep

What Animal
am I?

TIGER

U

I am a Mythical animal

I look like a big colorful horse

I have a horn on my head

What Mythical Animal am I?

UNICORN

V

I am very small like
a hamster

I have a longer, hair tail,
round head with small
ears and eyes

My name sounds like
"mole" but starts with
a "v"

What Animal
am I?

VOLE

W

I am **VERY** large and swim in the oceans

I have a blowhole on my head that lets me breathe air

I was named Moby in a book

What Animal am I?

WHALE

X

I am in the fish family

I live mostly in the
Amazon River

I have "see- through"
skin so you can see my
bones just like an Xray

What Animal
am I?

XRAY FISH

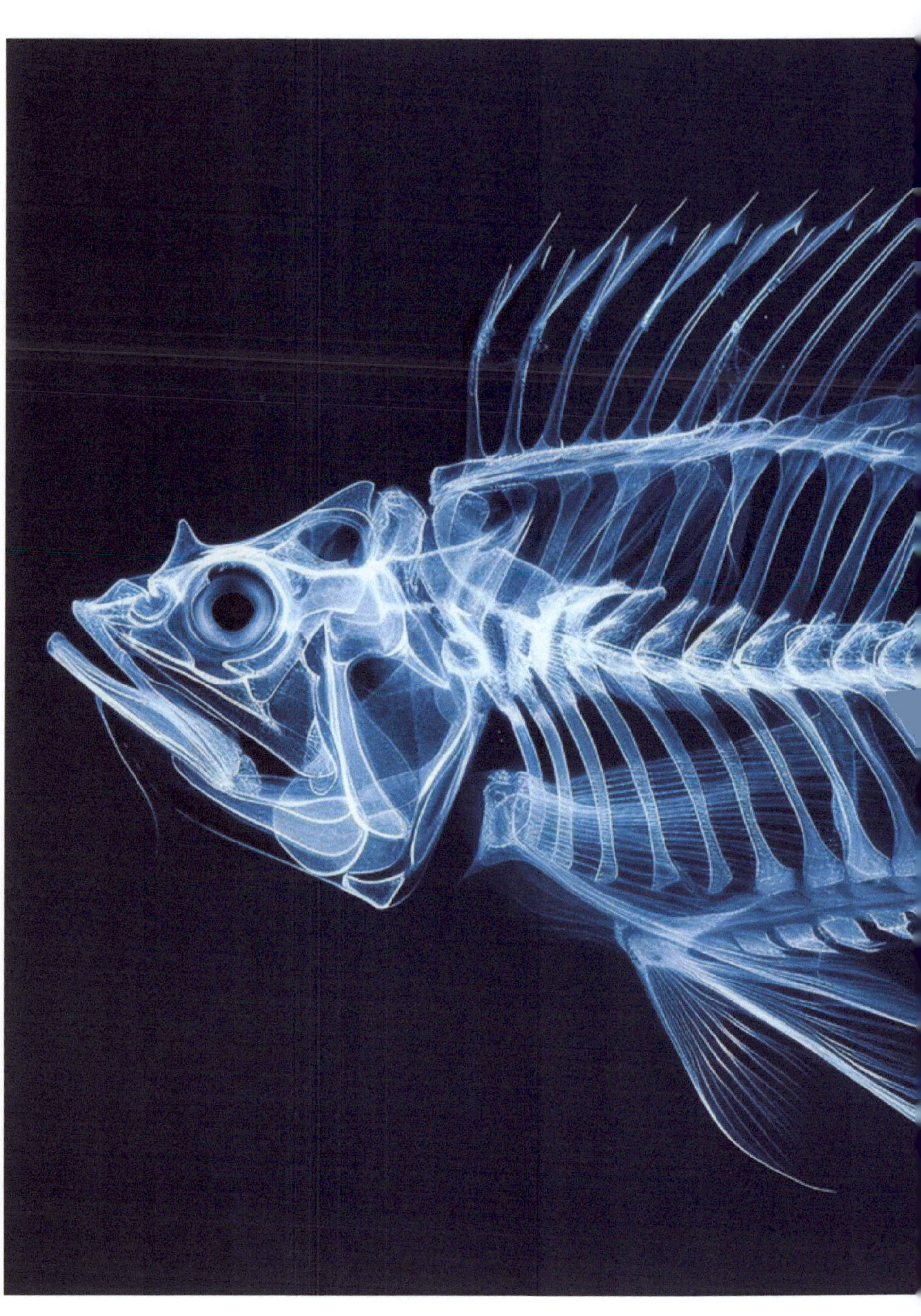

Y

I am in the cattle family

I have long hair, big horns
and cloven hooves

I live mostly in China and
Tibet

What Animal
am I?

YAK

Z

I look like a donkey or
small horse

I have black and
white stripes

I live mostly in the
grasslands or mountains
of Africa

What Animal
am I?

ZEBRA

Animal	Dreamstime ID	Copyright/Website purchased from
Alligator	6855800	© Isselee/Dreamstime.com
Beaver	306402842	© Sf1nks/Dreamstime.com
Cat	335668654	© Vitalybut/Dreamstime.com
Dog	145313708	© InnaKudasheya/Dreamstime.com
Elephant	3344027	© Isselee/Dreamstime.com
Flamingo	294333831	© Muhammadzubair/Dreamstime.com
Giraffe	360421804	© LiudmylaMazur/Dreamstime.com
Hippo	306593481	© SergheiStarus/Dreamstime.com
Iguana	16337236	© Dwiptra18/Dreamstime.com
Jaguar	317453997	© WasanPrunglampoo/Dreamstime.com
Kangaroo	338107697	© Yaroslaf/Dreamstime.com
Lion	356638286	© LyudmilaSoloveva/Dreamstime.com
Meerkat	362648276	© TatsianaKuryanovich/Dreamstime.com
Newt	129934442	© Isselee/Dreamstime.com
Ostrich	38943509	© Attaphong/Dreamstime.com
Porcupine	2894675	© Isselee/Dreamstime.com
Quail	66140003	© VasylHelevachuk/Dreamstime.com
Rat	28838135	© Viter8/Dreamstime.com
Snake	20377000	© Isselee/Dreamstime.com
Tiger	146398806	© SarayutThaneerat/Dreamstime.com
Unicorn	278096543	© IrynaZostrozhnova/Dreamstime.com
Vole	265743220	© Rudmer Zwerver/Dreamstime.com
Whale	355601895	© DzmitryAuramchik/Dreamstime.com
Xray Fish	347831731	© AndrilZorii/Dreamstime.com
Yak	6856320	© Isselee/Dreamstime.com
Zebra		Pinclipart.com_small=group=dip-art_5377222

B. Papa
Generated 2/27/25
Copyrighted pictures purchased through Dreamstime